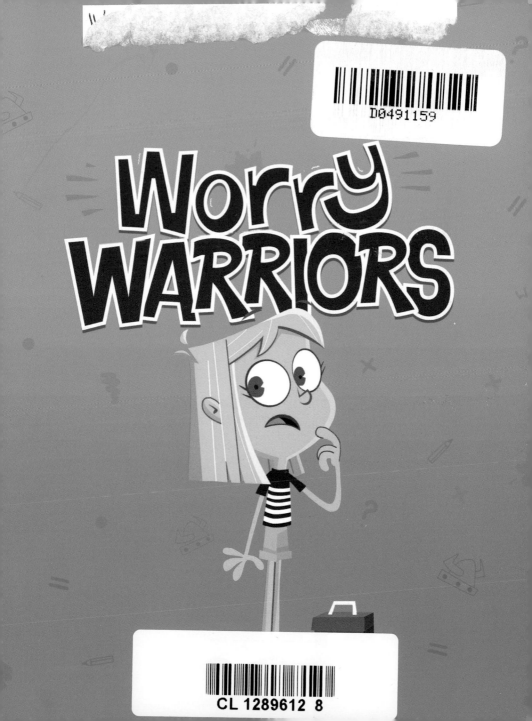

# Worry WARRIORS

Raintree is an imprint of Capstone Global Library Limited, a company incorporated in England and Wales having its registered office at 264 Banbury Road, Oxford, OX2 7DY – Registered company number: 6695582

www.raintree.co.uk
myorders@raintree.co.uk

Editor: Michelle Bisson
Designer: Hilary Wacholz

ISBN 978 1 4747 2846 1 (paperback)
20 19 18 17 16
10 9 8 7 6 5 4 3 2 1

British Library Cataloguing in Publication Data
A full catalogue record for this book is available from the British Library.

Printed and bound in China.

# Worry WARRIORS

## Nervous Nellie Fights First-day Frenzy

by Marne Ventura
illustrated by Leo Trinidad

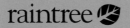
raintree

a Capstone company — publishers for children

# CONTENTS

Chapter 1
Class lists.................................................11

Chapter 2
Shmopping.............................................. 18

Chapter 3
Don't worry! Be happy! .......................... 27

Chapter 4
Room twelve..........................................35

Chapter 5
Heebie jeebies........................................43

Chapter 6
Day before the first...............................53

Chapter 7
**First day at last**...................................**59**

Chapter 8
**Mr Meaney**..........................................**66**

Chapter 9
**Rat monitor**.......................................**74**

Chapter 10
**Lost rat** ...........................................**80**

Chapter 11
**Best first day ever** ...........................**87**

# Worry WARRIORS

My name is Nellie Davis. I love to read, write, and play word games. Mum and Dad say I have an active imagination. That's great because when I grow up I want to be a writer. But it wasn't so great when I used to be scared of the dark and I imagined things like my toys coming to life and attacking me.

Luckily, my three absolute best friends ever live on my street. We've gone to school together since pre-school. And it turns out we all worry about something. And then we work together to help one another out.

Estella is an expert on movies and TV shows. She knows the names of all the actors, especially the kids. She loves dancing and cheerleading. She also likes hanging out with her family.

Jake loves to read, like I do. He's good at maths, science and computers. He wants to be a scientist one day. He's saving up for a robot racing car.

Adam is awesome at sport, art, and building projects. He has dyslexia. That means he learns to read, write and spell differently from most kids.

## WORRY WARRIORS UNITE

The best thing about my friends? I'm not the only one who worries. I found that out a few years back ...

One day, Estella, Adam, Jake and I were in my back garden making giant hula-hoop bubbles. We were running around barefoot on the wet grass. Estella almost stepped on a bee. She screamed so loudly that the lifeguards at the beach probably heard her. Then she ran inside. She wouldn't move an inch until Adam scooped up the bee with a plastic cup and put it into the bin. And put the lid on. Tight.

So then Estella said she felt silly, being scared of teeny little bees. But that she felt better after she had told us because we didn't laugh at her.

I didn't want Estella to feel silly alone, so I got up the nerve to tell my babyish secret: that I was afraid of the dark.

Then Adam said he gets scared walking across the bridge that goes over the dual carriageway. He holds on super-tight to his mum's hand and tries not to look down.

Jake told us he was afraid to wade into the sea because he could feel slimy stuff with his feet. What if he stepped on a poisonous jellyfish?

After we told each other our worries, we felt better. We didn't make fun of each other, like some kids would. And we realized that if all of us had secret worries, maybe they weren't so silly after all.

That's when I had the best idea ever! I asked my friends if they wanted to form a club. First we would tell each other our worries. Then together we would fight them, like knights and warrior princesses in shining armour!

And that's how we became the Worry Warriors.

# Chapter 1

# Class lists

It's Monday morning, a week before school starts. Estella, Jake, and I are sitting on my front steps.

Three monarch butterflies drift across my garden and land on a eucalyptus tree.

"Pretty butterflies!" Estella raises her arms like wings.

"They always show up at back-to-school time," Jake says, pushing his glasses up onto the bridge of his nose.

"I've got butterflies in my stomach," I say. "I can't wait to find out who our teacher will be."

"Me, too!" says Estella.

"Hi!" Adam jogs up the steps and jumps to bat the wind chime.

I open the door and stick my head in. Dad is clickety-clacking on his keyboard.

I go inside, stand next to him, and wait. Dad writes computer programs. He has to work everything out in his head like a puzzle. If I interrupt him, he might forget a puzzle piece.

Dad stops typing. "What's up?"

"We're going to walk to school."

"Okay," he says. "Have you tidied up your room?"

"I will, as soon as I get back." I give him a hug and then rush outside. Oops, I forget to close the door quietly and it slams. "Sorry, Dad!"

Estella, Jake, and Adam are on the pavement.

Estella is practising a cheer. "V for victory!" Her long hair swings from side to side.

Adam runs ahead of us, then walks backwards.

"I'm excited about the first day of school!" I tell Jake. "I hope we get Ms Anderson."

I know Ms Anderson from break when she is on playground duty. She has short, dark, curly hair and wears dangly earrings.

Ms Wise was the other year 5 teacher. She retired at the end of last year.

"I guess a new teacher will take Ms Wise's place," says Jake.

"Whoever it is, I hope we don't get a lot of homework," says Adam.

"Me too," says Estella. "And I hope we do plays and shows." She curves her arms like a ballerina and twirls.

"I wonder if Ms Anderson still has a pet rat?" asks Jake.

Jake's sister, Amanda, was in Ms Anderson's class two years ago. That's how he knows about the pet rat.

"Yuck!" I say.

"I wish I could have a pet rat!" says Adam.

"I hope she lets us have lots of ICT time," says Jake.

"Henry told me that she likes jokes," I say. My big brother was in Ms Anderson's class five years ago. "He gave me a super-funny joke to use if I get to be register monitor – which I really want to be."

"What is it?" asks Adam.

"It's a secret. You have to wait until I say it in class."

"Oh, okay," Adam says, hopping over a crack in the pavement.

"I hope we get to actually *do* things on the first day," I say. "Like a science experiment, or reading our new books. It's boring to spend all day talking about the rules."

I take a deep breath of salty sea air and think about my perfect first day of school. I'll sit near Adam, Estella, and Jake, just like I have since pre-school. I'll like Ms Anderson and she'll like me. When I write a report all about my summer holidays, she'll notice that my special talent is creative writing.

As we turn the corner, I see some other children

standing in front of the Sea View Primary School office. The big window is covered with papers. Class lists!

We look both ways and walk across the road. Then we run as fast as we can. By the time we reach the office the other children have left.

My heart is pumping hard, partly from running, but mostly because I'm so excited to see my class list. I find Ms Anderson's page and read the names. I find Adam Brown, Estella Garcia, and Jacob Williams.

I can't find my name. It should be between Adam and Estella. I read it again. Not there.

"Yay!" says Estella. "There we are – Jake, Adam, me – wait a minute. Where's Nellie?"

"Uh-oh." Jake is pointing to a different piece of paper. "Look, Nellie."

I look. It's the other year 5 class list: *New Teacher: To Be Announced*.

A pit of worry forms in my tummy.

I read down the list. I see the names of other kids in my year – Antonio Rhigetti, Alexis Sweet, Bella Thomas. Then I see my name. Eleanor Davis. In between Ashley Campbell and Ernesto Fernandez.

Wow. I feel like I've just been knocked over by a big wave in the sea. This is really horrible, very awful news.

# Chapter 2

## Shmopping

The next day Mum doesn't have a class to teach.
She takes the morning off for our special back-to-school
shopping day. We do it every year. I call it shmopping, since
it's me and Mum shopping.

"Ready to shmop till we drop?" she asks when Dad
and I come home from our wog, which is a walk and a
jog. Mum is drinking coffee from her Monarch Grove
University mug and typing on her laptop.

"I guess." I slump into a kitchen chair and put my head
on the table.

The back door squeaks open and bangs shut, and Lucy
comes into the kitchen carrying her sleepover bag. "I'm
home," she says. "What's wrong with Nellie?"

I lift my head and look at my big sister: long, blonde ponytail, blue and grey T-shirt and shorts, grey trainers with blue laces. Lucy's a cheerleader at Monarch Secondary School. Last night was the cheerleader slumber party.

"I haven't got Ms Anderson," I tell her. "I've got the new teacher."

"Bummer!" Lucy pours herself a bowl of cereal. "Who else is in your class?"

"Nobody!" I exclaim.

"None of your friends?" She pours milk on her cereal.

"Only me," I say, sadly.

"That's awful," says Lucy. "Is it a mrs or a mr?"

"Huh? I've never had a mr before! I've always had a ms!" I say. "What if the new teacher is a mr?"

"Year 5 was the first year I had a mr teacher," Lucy says. "He was really grumpy. He's not at Sea View any more. I don't think he liked kids."

My stomach flip-flops like a seashell in the tide. What

if the new teacher is really grumpy? What if he doesn't like kids? I put my head down on the kitchen table again. "Mum! I feel sick!" I call out.

Mum gives me a pat on the back. "I know you wanted to be in Ms Anderson's class with your friends. But try to keep an open mind. You might really like the new teacher."

"And you'll make new friends," says Dad.

"I don't want new friends! I want old friends! And what if the new teacher doesn't like me?"

"Impossible," says Dad.

"You're very likeable," agrees Mum.

I try to keep an open mind like Mum said, but my open mind keeps letting in more worries. What if nobody wants to sit next to me? What if the new teacher is mean?

"Do you know what kind of lunchbox you want this year?" asks Mum, as we get into the car. She's trying to cheer me up. It works a little. I love new lunch boxes.

\* \* \* \*

When we get to the shopping mall, the car park is nearly full. We have to hunt around for a space. I wonder if any of my best friends are here, too.

"Lots of shoppers!" says Mum.

I link arms with Mum as we go in. I love the smell of chocolate chip cookies from Mrs Meadow's. I love new school stuff. I love to watch the people riding on the escalator, carrying shopping bags. I love having Mum all to myself. For a minute, I almost forget about the first day of school.

"Do you want to start at Glam Kids?" asks Mum.

"Look, Mum!" I point to two mannequins in the Glam Kids window. One has long, dark hair. She's wearing a sparkly T-shirt and her arms are up like a ballerina. The other has straight blonde hair and she's reading a book.

"It looks like you and Estella!" says Mum.

"I can't believe we're not in the same class this year," I tell Mum as we go inside. "And I'm worried about lunch. I don't think I'll get to sit with Estella, Jake, and Adam.

They'll have to sit at Ms Anderson's table, and I'll have to sit at the new teacher's table. I'll miss my friends."

"Well, there's still morning break," says Mum. "And lunch break."

Mum's good at making me feel better. She teaches psychology, which studies how people think, feel, and act, so it helps her cheer me up when I'm down.

Another reason I cheer up is that Glam Kids has so many cool outfits. Right away I see the one I want. Denim skinny jeans and a plum, check, flannel shirt. Mum says I should get some of the shorts and T-shirts that are on sale.

At Shoe Stop I get the prettiest plum ballet shoes ever. I want new sandals and trainers, too, but Mum says the ones I have still fit.

I find the perfect plum rucksack with a flower zip pull, and a matching plum flowered lunchbox at Carry All. As Mum and I are standing in the queue to pay, Alexis Sweet walks up. She's with her university-student nanny, as usual.

"You're not getting *that* rucksack, are you?" Alexis has

blonde curls and blue eyes.

"What?" I hand my stuff to Mum and step out of the queue to talk to her.

"I don't love that plum colour." Alexis's nanny is holding three big bags. "I've just got the best clothes at Southland's. I don't like the stuff at Glam Kids." She's looking at my Glam Kids bag.

"I – ," I don't know what to say. Alexis is so mean. But what if she's right? Is my new stuff not cool?

"How do you feel about having a new teacher?" I ask, so I don't have to worry about whether my new clothes are not as cool as I think.

"No way I'm getting a new teacher. Daddy's going to call the principal and get me moved to Ms Anderson's," she says, and turns to leave.

Mum comes back from paying. "Poor girl," she says, as we watch Alexis and her nanny leave the shop.

"Mum, she's totally rich," I say.

"I meant unfortunate," says Mum. "I never see her with

her parents. Or with friends."

"Not having friends is her own fault," I say.

Mum just shakes her head.

I try not to think about Alexis as we pick out plum-flowered notebooks, pencils, and markers at Paper Palace. I just want to have fun with Mum.

"That's everything," says Mum after we pay. "Let's get lunch."

We share a turkey, avocado, and tomato sandwich at Pacific Café. Then at Fro Yo Heaven we get vanilla bean frozen yoghurt with brownie chunks, slivered almonds, hot fudge, and whipped cream.

Part of me is having fun shmopping with Mum. But part of me can't stop feeling nervous about the first day of school. "Mum," I ask, as we look for a table in the food court. "Can Alexis's dad really tell the principal to move her to Ms Anderson's class? Could you do the same for me?"

"I don't know about Alexis," says Mum. "But Sea View Primary is a great school. The teachers put pupils into the class they think is best for them. They probably have a good reason for placing you in the new teacher's class."

We sit at a little round table to eat our frozen yoghurt and watch the shoppers go by. I jiggle my legs as I think about the first day of school.

"Try to relax, Nervous Nellie," Mum smiles and squeezes my hand. "Stay in the here-and-now. Aren't we having a good time?"

"Shmopping is super fun," I tell Mum. "But can you homeschool me this year?"

# Chapter 3

# Don't worry! Be happy!

Mum says instead of being homeschooled, I should have an emergency Worry Warriors meeting. So when we get back from shmopping, I call Jake, Adam, and Estella. They promise to come over the next morning.

We meet in my back garden tree house. Dad and Henry built it when Henry was little. This year, Henry's starting secondary school. He's busy doing secondary school stuff like being on the athletics team, so he doesn't mind if we use it.

Jake and Estella show up at ten o'clock. Adam comes in as we're putting on the Viking helmets that we got at the after-Halloween costume sale a couple of years ago. To start the meeting, we raise our right hands and yell "Don't worry! Be happy!"

"I hereby call this meeting to order," I say. "Let's start by saying what worries us about the first day of school."

"And remember," says Estella, "nobody is allowed to say someone's worry is stupid."

Jake nods. "No making fun, or laughing."

"Right," says Adam. "And, what happens in the tree house stays in the tree house."

I settle into a beanbag chair. "Who wants to go first?"

"I'm worried that I won't get my schoolwork done during lesson time," says Adam, "and I'll have to finish it after school instead of going outside to play football. And, this is stupid, but I worry that I'll get lost and won't be able to find the toilet or my new classroom."

"I'm afraid I've forgotten my times tables over the summer," says Estella. "What if I don't even make it into the lowest maths group?"

"I hate it when nobody wants to pick me for their team in gym," says Jake.

"I don't want a new teacher," I say. "What if she's mean,

or strict, or doesn't like me? What if it's a he? And I won't have any friends! Who will I sit next to? Who will I eat lunch with? What if the other children in my class don't like me?" I stop, exhausted and scared.

"Wow," says Estella. "We have a lot of worries."

"I guess we should work on a plan to fight them," I say.

"*En garde*, worries!" says Adam. He picks up one of the cardboard swords and shields that we made last summer, and starts to duel with Jake.

"Take that!" yells Jake, stabbing his sword into Adam's shield.

"Knock it off, you two," says Estella.

"Let's brainstorm ideas," I say.

"Let's run away." Adam drops his sword and shield. "We'll camp out at the beach. Then we won't have to go to school at all."

"I'd miss TV," says Estella. "And my mum."

"I'd miss the library," I say.

"Let's ask our mums to move us to a different school," says Jake, "where we can be in the same class together. A school where every child gets his own tablet."

"Or," says Estella, "we could pretend to be sick on the first day of school."

"We could be drop-outs!" I say.

Just then Dad knocks on the door and comes in with a big bowl of strawberries. "Any hungry warriors around? How's it going?"

"We have a lot of worries," I tell him. "So we're thinking of ways to get out of going to the first day of school."

"Hmmm," says Dad. "Why not come up with a plan to make the first day of school better?"

After Dad leaves, we eat strawberries while we talk some more about what to do.

"I think Dad is right," I say. "We're not going to get out of the first day of school. Does anyone have any ideas to make it better?"

We all eat some more strawberries and think hard.

"Let's go to school and practise walking around," says Jake. "So we're sure we know where our new classrooms are. And the toilets!"

"Sounds good," I say, trying not to laugh about the toilets. We promised not to laugh at each other's fears.

"Also, you know you can practise football with me," Adam tells Jake. "And if I'm team captain, I'll pick you."

"We can practise making new friends," says Estella.

"I can test you on your times tables," I tell her.

"You can ask the teacher for audiobooks," Estella tells Adam. "That helped you get your work done last year."

"Sounds like a plan," says Adam. "Meeting over! Let's have a water balloon war!"

We raise our hands and yell, "Don't worry! Be happy!"

Then we go outside and fill the balloons that Adam brought. We run around and throw them at each other until we're out of breath. I'm wet and drippy, and my sides ache from laughing. I feel better about the first day of school.

When Dad says it's time to clean up, we put all the pieces of broken balloons in the bin. My friends have to go home for lunch. I go inside and change into dry clothes. I look at my back-to-school stuff. Then my open mind starts to worry again.

What if my new stuff is not cool? Should I have picked a different rucksack and lunchbox? Did I get too much plum flowered stuff?

Maybe I'll still drop out.

# Chapter 4

# Room twelve

The next morning, as we walk to school to practise finding our way around, I test Estella on her times tables.

"Eight times two," I say.

Estella counts on her fingers.

"Estella, just count in twos," says Jake. "Two-four-six-eight …"

"Oh, sixteen," says Estella.

"You can use the same trick for fives," I tell her. "What's five times three?"

"Five-ten-fifteen!" she exclaims.

"See? It's not that hard!" says Jake.

Estella twirls around the lamp-post and kicks up one leg as we wait at the crossing.

"Or maybe it's easy for you because you like maths," Adam says to Jake.

"I do like maths," says Jake. He runs his hand over his hair. He's just had a back-to-school haircut. "Do you guys think it's weird to like maths? Because sometimes I feel like other children think that."

"It's not weird," says Adam. "People just like different things. Everyone has a special thing they like." He pushes his hair out of his eyes.

"I know what you mean," I tell Jake. "Sometimes children act like it's weird that I want to read so much."

"Being good at something makes it fun," says Estella, "And you and Jake are good at school."

"Reading is hard for me," says Adam. "I'd rather be outside playing sports." He kicks a rock all the way across the pavement.

"Reading's okay, but maths is hard for me," says Estella.

"It's more fun to do something I'm good at, like dancing. And homework is a pain, because Mum won't let me watch TV until it's done."

"I hate that, too," says Adam.

"I'd do extra homework if I could be in Ms Anderson's class with you," I tell my friends.

We reach the school office and find our class lists again. Ms Anderson's class is in Room Eleven. New Teacher is in Room Twelve.

"At least we'll be right next door to you," says Estella as we walk to our classrooms.

We stand on our tiptoes and press our faces against Ms Anderson's window.

"Cool noticeboards," says Estella.

"There's a bin with sport stuff," says Adam.

I look around. One noticeboard is covered with ocean blue paper. Across the top it says *My Super Summer*. There are cartoon pictures of a boy surfing and a girl jumping off a diving board.

I sigh. If only I were in Ms Anderson's class, my report on my summer holiday would get pinned up there.

The next note is covered with plum paper, my favourite colour! At the top it says *Room Eleven Monitors*. There are cartoon pictures of pencils, paper, erasers, and books. If only I were in Ms Anderson's class, my name might be pinned up there next to Register Monitor.

"Look!" says Estella. "Costumes!"

In the back corner there's a bin full of sparkly and furry clothes, a firefighter's helmet, and a princess tiara.

"I bet she's going to do plays and shows!" Estella says.

"I see a set of tablets on the back counter!" says Jake.

"Bummer, I don't see a pet rat anywhere," says Adam. "I was really hoping for a pet rat."

"I was really hoping for NO rat," I tell Adam. "But I guess it doesn't matter, since I'm not in this class anyway."

I feel the way I did last year when Grace invited everyone but me to her birthday party. It was horrible. But when Estella asked Grace why she didn't invite me, she said she did. She found the invitation in the bottom of her rucksack. It was just a mistake.

But I am definitely NOT on Ms Anderson's class list. It isn't a mistake. My three best friends in the world will be doing all kinds of fun stuff in Room Eleven and I'll be in Room Twelve. Even though our rooms are next to each other, I feel like I'll be a gazillion miles away.

"Let's go see your room, Nellie." Estella hooks her arm in mine and we walk to the next classroom.

I stand on my toes and press my face against the window. The glass feels cool and hard. Chairs are stacked up in one corner, and tables are pushed together in another corner. The noticeboards are empty.

It looks like the caretaker has swept the floor and made a pile of paper scraps and dirt in the middle of the room, but then didn't scoop it up.

There are cardboard boxes stacked along one side of the room. They're marked on the side: *Reading, Art, Science, Maths.*

Then I see two things that make my stomach drop like a crashing wave.

A note is taped to the teacher's desk at the front of the room. It says MR MEANEY.

On the floor next to the desk, there's a rat cage.

Chapter 5

# Heebie jeebies

On the walk home, I tell Estella, Jake, and Adam how much rats give me the creeps. We decide to go to the pet shop the next day to practise being around a rat.

In the morning, Dad says he'll walk us to Cute Critters as soon as I've tidied my room. I call my friends and tell them I'll be ready in an hour.

Then I go into my room and look around.

It's not that bad. There are some books and clothes on the floor and under the bed. And on the bottom of my wardrobe. Papers, magazines, and books are covering my desk. And sticking out of my drawers. Stuffed animals are everywhere. I used to collect them, but I don't play with them any more.

Under my bed, I discover a library book I haven't read. It's from one of my favourite mystery series! I sit down to read, just for a minute.

Dad comes and stands in the doorway. "Why are you reading instead of tidying? And, are those *library* books in your basket? I hope they're not overdue."

I hop up and pull the books out of the basket. "We can take them back after we go to Cute Critters," I tell him. You'd think he'd be happy I like to read so much!

"Now that school is starting," says Dad, "it's important to have a tidy room. You don't want to be late because you can't find something, do you?"

"I hadn't thought of that! What if I'm late for school? What if I'm late on the *first day*?" I drop the stack of books I'd just picked up. They scatter on the floor.

Dad comes in and helps me pick up the books. "You won't be late, because you're going to get everything tidied up. Right, Nervous Nellie?" He smiles and gives me a rub on the head.

"I don't know what it will be like to have Mr Meaney," I tell Dad. "I've never had a mr teacher before. Lucy said the first mr teacher she had was grumpy and didn't like kids."

"But last year, Lucy's teacher was Mr Alan. He was her favourite teacher ever," says Dad.

"True."

"I'm a mr," says Dad, "and I'm pretty nice."

I laugh and give Dad a hug.

"Instead of thinking of how things could go wrong, try thinking of *good* things that might happen." Dad looks at his watch. "Your friends will be here in 45 minutes. Can you get your room tidied by then?"

"Yes!" I say. Then I tidy up my room, super-fast.

Dad checks it over and gives me a thumbs up.

I hear a knock and run to open the door for Estella and Jake.

"Everyone here?" asks Dad.

I see Adam jogging up the pavement. "Yep! Let's go."

We walk the short walk to Cute Critters on Beach Street. A groomer is brushing a white, fluffy puppy in the salon. It's so cute and furry. It looks up at me and wags its tail.

"Dogs are lucky," I say. "They don't have to worry about new teachers."

"Or reading," says Adam.

"Or maths," says Estella.

"Or gym," says Jake.

It smells like dogs and wood shavings in Cute Critters. A man with big glasses and a Cute Critter badge asks, "Can I help you?"

"Do you have rats?" asks Estella.

He waves his hand for us to follow him to the back corner of the shop. There are rats in cages along the wall.

"Can I hold one?" asks Adam.

"Of course," says the man. He helps Adam open a cage and pick up a rat.

Estella asks to hold a rat, too.

Dad and Jake are busy looking at an app that's on Dad's iPhone.

I stand back.

"Why don't you like rats?" asks Adam. He's holding a big black rat with brown eyes. He lifts it up and the rat sniffs his chin. Its long whiskers wiggle.

"Remember that movie we watched, where all those rats were swimming around in the sewer? With beady red eyes? In the dark?"

"It was just a movie," says Adam.

"And their tails!" I point at Estella's rat. It has a long, pink, scaly, creepy tail. It freaks me out!

"Rats are quite intelligent," the Cute Critters man says. "They make great pets because they're so friendly. You can teach them tricks. They're loyal, and very clean."

Adam is letting the rat sit on his shoulder. "Want to hold this one?"

I shake my head no. I want to run out of the pet shop! If the new teacher has pet rats, I'm definitely dropping out of school. I am never going to touch a rat. NEVER.

I'm glad when Dad says, "Let's move on to the library, kids. I need to get back to work soon."

We thank the Cute Critters man for his help and walk around the corner to the library.

"Do you really think the new teacher's name is Mr Meaney?" I ask.

"Names don't tell you anything," says Jake. "How about Alexis Sweet?"

"True," I say. "Alexis is NOT sweet. She's as mean as a shark. Still, it seems like a bad sign. Who wants a teacher named Mr Meaney?"

"Yeah," says Jake. "I'd definitely rather have Mr Cool, or Mr Awesome, or at least Mr Nice."

"Sometimes I think Alexis wants to be friends with us," says Adam.

I can't believe my friends are not agreeing with me.

"Me, too," says Estella. "It's like she just doesn't know *how* to be nice. Maybe she needs some help."

Hmm. If my friends think this, and my Mum does too, maybe I should consider it, too. But. Not. Right. Now. I have books to return.

At the library after I return my books we stop at the noticeboard by the front door. It says WHAT DID YOU DO THIS SUMMER? There are photographs of people swimming with dolphins, standing by castles, jet skiing, bungee jumping, flying in jets, and climbing mountains.

As we're about to leave, Alexis comes in. Her nanny is carrying a stack of books. I didn't realize Alexis liked to read. She probably reads about how to be better than anyone else. When she opens her mouth, I think I'm right.

"*I* went to Disney World in Florida for *my* summer holiday," she says. "It was the best."

"Jeez," says Jake, as Alexis disappears into the library.

"See what I mean?" says Estella. "She doesn't know how to talk to people. She didn't even say hello."

"Weird," says Adam.

I don't want to talk about it. It's bad enough that she's going to be in my class and she did something way better than me this summer. Maybe she *is* better than anyone else.

"What am I going to write for my summer holiday report?" I ask as we walk home. "I didn't do anything great." Every year since year 2, we've had to write a summer holiday report on the first day of school. I don't think that will change this year, whoever teaches my class.

"You're good at creative writing," says Estella. "Make something up."

"How about this?" I ask. " 'My Super Summer Holiday, by Nellie Davis. This summer, I travelled across the country alone to spend a week with my grandparents. They live in an ivy-covered mansion on a beautiful lake. Whilst on an archaeological dig, I discovered a long-lost treasure of great historical value.' "

"Cool," says Adam.

"Awesome," says Jake.

"Super-creative," says Estella.

"Well," says Dad, "That *is* an exciting way to say I drove you an hour away to Grandma and Grandpa's little house on the golf course and you found Grandma's lost necklace in the back garden."

"Too much?" I ask.

"Maybe," says Dad.

This makes my stomach all jumbly, so I try to stop thinking about the first day of school. Mr Meaney, pet rats, my summer holiday report; everything about it gives me the heebie jeebies.

## Chapter 6

# Day before the first

On Sunday I get ready for the first day of school. I take the tags off my rucksack and lunchbox. I pick out a notebook, pen, and pencil.

Mum comes in to see how it's going.

I'm laying out my new long-sleeved outfit.

"It's really been warm lately," she says. "Those are a lovely pair of jeans and shirt, but I'm afraid you'll be uncomfortably hot."

"But this is my best new outfit," I say. "I really want to wear it tomorrow."

"It's your decision," says Mum. "I just want you to think it through. You do have some new shorts and T-shirts.

You could save that outfit to wear for when the weather gets cooler."

Mum has a point. Last year I practically died of the heat on the first day of school because I wore my new warm clothes. And right now I'm wearing shorts and a vest top and I'm still warm. But I really like my new outfit!

I look at my other new clothes. They're cool too. I lay out the denim shorts and the plum and white striped T-shirt. But then I worry, will I fit in with the other kids in my classroom?

I call Estella and her mum says she can come over. She gets here in five minutes!

"I can't decide what to wear tomorrow," I tell her. "Usually we plan what to wear together – but now we're not in the same class."

"Let's wear the same thing, anyway," says Estella. "I'm going to wear denim shorts and a pink T-shirt with sparkle stripes. It's been pretty warm lately."

I show her my outfit and we laugh.

"We picked out almost the same thing without talking about it!" It makes me feel better to know that Estella and I will have matching clothes, even if we're not wearing them in the same classroom.

Then I feel sad about not being together.

"Are you bringing packed lunch or having school dinner?" I ask Estella.

"Packed lunch," says Estella. "I want to use my new lunchbox."

"Me, too. What are you going to eat?"

"I don't know yet."

"Let's make our lunches match, like our clothes!" I tell Estella. "Want to bring cheese and crackers, baby carrots, and strawberries?"

"Okay," says Estella. "And a hard-boiled egg."

"And Mum's making chocolate chip cookies today, so I'll bring one for you!"

"But," says Estella, "we won't be sitting together at

lunch since we're not in the same class." She looks sad too. I suddenly want to cry, but manage not to.

 "I'll give you a cookie to put in your lunch before you go home."

"Hey," says Estella, "We haven't practised how to make new friends."

I feel super-sad now. I don't want a new friend. I want Estella to be in my classroom.

"Pretend that I'm sitting at the desk next to you," says Estella. She sits down at my desk and picks up a book. "How are you going to make friends with me?"

I tap Estella on the shoulder and say, "Hi, I'm Nellie. What's your name?"

"Estella."

Now I don't know what to say!

"You like to read," says Estella. "Ask me about the book in my hand."

"Oh – good idea!" I look at the book Estella's holding.

"I read that book this summer. Do you like it?"

"Yes! I've got the whole series at home."

Mum knocks on the door. "Anyone need a cookie break?"

Estella and I both yell, "I do!"

I feel happy, eating cookies and drinking milk with Estella. But, I also feel worried about tomorrow. If I find a new friend, will Estella find a new friend too? What if Estella doesn't need me for a friend any more?

# Chapter 7

## First day at last

I can't fall asleep on Sunday night. I check my alarm clock a million times, and get up twice to remind Mum and Dad to make sure I'm up on time. I guess I finally fall asleep, because the next thing I remember is waking up from a bad dream two minutes before my alarm clock is about to ring.

Mum comes into my room and sits on my bed. "Ready for school?"

"No! I just dreamed that I was standing in front of my class. The kids were all staring at me. The only one I recognized was Alexis, and she was glaring at me. I was supposed to be giving a presentation, but I hadn't written it. And I was still wearing my pyjamas! I turned to the teacher, and he was the man at Cute Critters. A big, white rat with red eyes was hunched on his shoulder."

"That sounds scary," says Mum. "But it was just a dream, right?"

"Yes, it was just a dream," I repeat.

"And you will know a lot of the kids in your class, even if they're not your best friends," says Mum.

"I do like Ashley and Ernesto. They're in my class," I say.

"And have you ever *not* been ready for a presentation?" asks Mum.

I smile. "No, I always work hard on my presentations."

Mum gives me a hug. "Dad's making happy face toast."

Dad has made me a special breakfast on my first day of school ever since reception. First he toasts a slice of bread. Then he spreads it with peanut butter and makes a happy face using banana slices with a blueberry in the centre for the eyes, half a strawberry for the nose, and a curvy line of raisins for the mouth.

I get dressed and go to the kitchen. The coffee and toast smell good. I take a sip of milk and look at my breakfast. My stomach feels all jiggly, like a jellyfish. I don't feel hungry at all.

"You're not getting too old for happy face toast, are you?" asks Dad.

"Never. But I wish I could have one more day of summer," I tell him. "We'd be wogging on the beach right now."

"I like our wogs, too," says Dad. "But give school a chance. Think about it – have you ever *not* liked school before?"

I take a nibble of toast. "I've always liked school before," I say. "But what if I don't like it now?"

"Wait and see," says Dad. "You might be happily surprised."

I pull off a blueberry eye, but I just can't eat.

In a few minutes Estella and Jake knock at the front door. Estella's hair is in a French plait, and Jake has new glasses. Then Adam jogs up. He looks really nice in his new shirt.

"Ready?" asks Estella.

"Yes!" Seeing my friends makes me feel better. I run into the kitchen, give Mum and Dad a hug, and grab my rucksack.

The first day of school feels less scary with Estella, Jake, and Adam walking with me. It's a warm, sunny day.

Ms O'Dell is waiting for us at the corner in her lollipop lady's outfit. "Look how grown-up you are!"

"Hi, Ms O!" We all slap high-fives.

The front of the school is crowded with kids. I walk with Estella, Jake, and Adam to Room Eleven and they put down their rucksacks. They walk with me to Room Twelve and I put down my rucksack.

We go out to the playground together, but before we have a chance to do anything, the bell rings and it's time to line up. Estella, Jake, and Adam give me a thumbs-up and rush to their room. I walk slowly to Room Twelve.

My heart is pounding!

"Hi, Nellie." Ernesto is first in line.

"Hi, Ernesto," I reply.

A new girl gets in the line behind me. She looks worried.

"Hi," I say. "I'm Nellie. Are you new?"

"Yes, I'm Brittany. I've just moved here," she says.

I wonder if Brittany is more nervous than I am.

Ashley gets in line behind Brittany.

"Hi, Ashley. Where's Grace?" I ask.

"Ms Anderson's," says Ashley.

I make a sad face to show Ashley I'm sorry she and her best friend aren't in the same class this year.

More children join the line. I know most of them, but a few are new. I'm surprised – and not very happy – to see Alexis get in the line.

I'm worried that this is going to be an even worse, more horrible first day than I thought.

I hear Ms Anderson greeting her class next door. I watch Estella, Jake, and Adam go inside with the rest of their classmates.

Suddenly the hallway is quiet. I feel all jittery, shaky, and hoppy. Then the classroom door swings open.

# Chapter 8

●

# Mr Meaney

A man with red hair comes through the door. He's wearing blue jeans and running shoes, a button-down shirt and tie. He looks younger than Dad.

"Welcome," he says. "Please come in and find your seat. Your rucksacks go on the pegs in the cloakroom."

I put my rucksack away, and find my nametag on a desk near the front.

I look around the classroom. Mr Meaney has done a lot since I peeked in the window a few days ago!

One corner of the room has three beanbags on a rug. The walls are lined with shelves full of books. And they're not schoolbooks, they're free reading books! That makes me happy.

What doesn't make me happy is that the cage is still there. Now it's on the back shelf with a big, grey rat in it. The water fountain and the pencil sharpener are at the end of the shelf. I'm going to always bring sharpened pencils from home. Extras. And I will never get a drink of water there, not even if I have salty crisps in my lunch.

"Let's get to know each other," says Mr Meaney. "I'll start. My name is Mr Meaney, but I'm not mean. I'm nice."

We all laugh.

"The name Meaney comes from an old Irish word that means wealthy. And I have lots of money! This is Meaney money." He pulls a rectangle of paper from a pile of pound-note-sized papers. He hands the stack to Brittany. "Will you please give one to each student?"

Mr Meaney points to a chart on the wall that tells how much you earn for different things. It's really cool! We can earn Meaney money by handing in work on time, doing monitor jobs, and following class rules.

Brittany hands me a note. It's made with a photocopier. In the centre, where there's usually a picture of the queen, there's a picture of Mr Meaney's face. I'm puzzled, but it makes me smile.

Ernesto is raising his hand.

"Yes?" says Mr Meaney.

"I don't think we can use these at the shops," he says.

The children laugh.

"You're right," says Mr Meaney. "But in Room Twelve, you can use Meaney money to buy free time. During free time, you can use the reading corner, do special art projects or science experiments, or spend time with the rat. You can even use Meaney money for a free pass if you forget your homework or aren't ready for a spelling test. But only once."

"What's that?" Alexis asks, without raising her hand. She's pointing to the noticeboard at the side of the room. It's where teachers usually put the summer holiday reports, but this one says *Hall of Fame* across the top.

"You're going to write an *All About Me* report," says Mr Meaney. "I'll put it on the *Hall of Fame* noticeboard. It will help us get to know each other. Your parents will read your reports at parents' evening. I'd like you to work on your *All About Me* page now, and then we'll choose classroom monitors."

"Can I write about my trip to Disney World?" asks Alexis.

"It's not a summer holiday report," says Mr Meaney.

Alexis sticks out her lower lip and crosses her arms. I would almost feel sorry for her if she wasn't always so "I'm all that."

Mr Meaney writes the directions on the board as he talks. "Write a list of at least ten things that tell us who you are, what you like, what you're good at, and also what you don't like and are not good at. Be honest."

I get right to work.

## ALL ABOUT NELLIE DAVIS.

### 1. I am nine years old.

2. I have straight, blonde hair and hazel eyes.

3. I live with my family in Monarch Grove.

4. My friends are Estella, Jake and Adam.

5. I have a good imagination.

6. Usually I'm happy, but sometimes I worry.

7. My favourite colour is plum and strawberries are my favourite things to eat.

8. I like free reading, creative writing and science experiments.

9. I also like walking and jogging on the beach with my dad (wogging) and shopping with my Mum (shmopping).

10. My favourite books are *Charlotte's Web*, *Marvin Redpost*, *Ramona*, *Harry Potter* and *Anastasia*.

11. When I grow up, I plan to be a famous writer.

12. I'm not very good at keeping my room tidy.

13. I'm afraid of rats.

I stop and chew on the end of my pencil. Is it okay to say I don't like rats? Maybe I'm supposed to like them.

I rub out the last sentence.

But then Mr Meaney says, "Please finish up. I'd like to choose monitors before break."

He writes on the whiteboard:

*Ball Monitor*

*Paper Monitor*

*Art Monitor*

Some of the kids are already raising their hands to volunteer for the jobs.

"Hands down for now," says Mr Meaney. "Let's talk about responsibility."

I look at my *All About Me* page. It looks messy and smudgy where I rubbed stuff out. I try rubbing out the smudge, but I make a hole in the paper. I really want it to be good. I decide to start again on clean paper. I can keep working on it and listen to Mr Meaney at the same time. I really hope I get picked for register monitor!

I concentrate on using my absolute best handwriting. I'm working so hard that I forget to listen. When I hear Mr Meaney say "register" I raise my hand high.

"All right, Nellie. You'll be rat monitor."

I drop my hand and look around. What happened? Didn't he just say register?

On the whiteboard, it now says

*Rat Monitor*

*Register Monitor*

*Window Monitor*

I must have raised my hand too soon! Why wasn't I paying attention?

I have made a total mess of everything.

This is the worst first day of school ever!

## Chapter 9

# Rat monitor

Mr Meaney dismisses us for morning break. He tells us to hand in our *All About Me* reports as we leave, but I don't, because I haven't finished copying it.

When I get outside, Estella, Jake and Adam are waiting for me.

"How was it?" asks Jake.

"I accidentally volunteered to be rat monitor!"

"Oh, no!" say Estella, Jake, and Adam together.

"Can't you tell Mr Meaney it was an accident?" asks Adam.

"Then I'll have to admit I wasn't listening," I say. "I was supposed to put away my report, but I kept working on it."

"That's bad," says Jake.

"Super-bad," says Estella.

"What are you going to do?" asks Adam.

"I'm going to have to take care of the rat." I feel all creepy and itchy. "It's a big, fat, grey one."

"Stay calm," says Adam. "Remember what the pet shop guy said? Rats are smart, loyal, and clean. You can do it!"

"I don't know," I say.

"Is Mr Meaney mean?" asks Estella.

"No, he seems super-nice. How's Ms Anderson?"

"Good!" say Jake, Adam and Estella together.

"She doesn't make kids stay in at break to finish work," says Adam. "She thinks it's important to get outside and move around."

"And guess what?" says Jake. "We're going to the ICT room for reports and research. And games, if we earn free time."

"And we're doing a play for the performance just before Christmas!" says Estella.

I show Estella, Jake and Adam my Meaney money. I tell them about the awesome free reading corner, free-time art and science projects, and the homework and spelling test pass. They say Mr Meaney sounds like a fun teacher.

Then the bell rings. Back to my rat monitor job. Yikes!

Estella, Jake and Adam walk me to my line. They give me a Worry Warrior knuckle tap for courage.

Inside, Mr Meaney says, "If you have a monitor job, please do it now."

I walk slowly back to the rat cage. There's a sign by the cage that says TEMPLETON. Mr Meaney named it after the rat in *Charlotte's Web*! There's also a sign on the wall that says:

RAT MONITOR DAILY DUTIES

CLEAN AND FILL THE FOOD DISH

CLEAN AND FILL THE WATER TUBE

I wiggle my shoulders to shake off the heebie jeebies. Then I take a closer look. The rat is curled up in a pile of wood shavings. It opens its eyes and looks at me. Its eyes *are* sort of intelligent-looking, like the pet shop guy said. They're black, not red eyes that glow in the dark.

The rat stands and stretches, then puts its front paws against the side of the cage and wiggles its nose at me. I'm glad I can't see its tail.

My heart is banging, hard. I take a deep breath.

I unlatch the door to the cage. I hope the rat will stay put in there.

But, it lowers its paws and moves towards the door. I jump back. My stomach flip-flops. How can I get it to stay in the corner?

Maybe I should tell Mr Meaney the truth. Will I get into trouble?

The rat sniffs its empty dish, then goes back to the wood shaving pile. It curls up and closes its eyes.

I take another deep breath and reach in for the dish.

The rat opens its eyes and stands up again.

I jump back.

"Class, I need your attention," Mr Meaney says.

I turn around to listen.

"We'll be doing our first science experiment on Wednesday."

Yay! I'll have to feed the rat later. I love science experiments! I wonder what this one will be? Mr Meaney is arranging papers on his desk.

I turn around to close the door before I go back to my desk.

What I see is very bad. The door is wide open. And the rat is gone.

# Chapter 10

# Lost rat

I look behind everything on the shelf and all around the floor. The rat is nowhere!

"Everyone seated, please," says Mr Meaney. "Nellie, do you need help with something?"

I stand up straight. My cheeks are burning.

"No, I'm okay," I say.

I go back to my desk. How am I going to find the rat and get it back to its cage?

"Pay attention, now," says Mr Meaney. He has some jars and bottles on his desk. "Has anyone heard of the scientific method?"

I know the answer, but I don't raise my hand.

I lean out from my desk and search the floor. Where is the rat?

Brittany turns around. "What are you looking for?" she whispers.

"I've lost the rat!" I whisper back. "Do you see it anywhere?"

Brittany lifts her feet, then looks under the desks in front of her.

Ashley and Ernesto must have heard too. They're looking all around.

"The scientific method is when you guess something, and then test your guess by trying it," says Alexis.

"Good," says Mr Meaney. "I need everyone's full attention," he adds.

I sit up. He's looking at me. My face feels hot.

Mr Meaney takes an egg from his desk and holds it up. "What would happen if I dropped this egg?"

"It would break," most of the children call out.

"I can't see the rat anywhere!" whispers Brittany.

"Neither can I," whispers Ernesto.

"What am I going to do?" I cry. "I've lost the rat!"

"The classroom door's open," whispers Ashley. "Did it go outside?"

What if the rat has gone outside? It might get squished by  a car, or eaten by a cat. I have to find it!

"But what if we do something to the egg to change the hard shell?" Mr Meaney asks. He points to a bottle of white vinegar and a jar on his desk.

I feel sick! I've lost the rat. I want to pay attention to Mr Meaney, but I can't. Where is the rat?

"I want each of you to make a hard-boiled egg at home tonight, and bring it to school tomorrow. We're going to soak our eggs in vinegar for a couple of days."

I lean over and search the floor again.

All at once, I hear kids whispering and giggling. I look up to see what's funny.

A tiny pink nose is poking up from the chair behind Mr Meaney's desk. Then two little paws reach up and grab the edge. Slowly, the rat pulls itself onto the desk and walks over to the egg. It stands with its front paws on the egg and sniffs the air, wiggling its whiskers.

The whole class is laughing like crazy.

"The rat's escaped!" yells Antonio.

"It wants to eat the egg!" squeals the girl behind Antonio.

"How did it get out?" asks the boy next to Brittany.

Mr Meaney looks at me, and raises an eyebrow. "Nellie?"

I sit up straight.

"Would you please put the rat back into its cage?" he asks.

I walk slowly up to Mr Meaney's desk. He's holding the rat in one hand now, against his chest. The rat is sniffing Mr Meaney's pocket.

My legs are wobbly. I can feel everyone staring at me.

"Are you okay?" Mr Meaney asks.

I don't think I can take the rat from Mr Meaney and put it back into its cage. What should I do? I take a deep breath and let it out. I have to tell Mr Meaney the truth.

"I'm afraid of rats," I say, super-quietly. "I didn't mean to let it out. I opened the cage door to feed it. But I was scared to put my hand in the cage. Then I turned around to listen to you. And it got out."

Mr Meaney is quiet for a second. "If you feel that way, why did you volunteer to be rat monitor?"

"I wanted to be register monitor," I say. "But I was trying to do a good job on my *All About Me* report, and I messed it up. So I was copying it out again, and not listening, and I raised my hand at the wrong time." I'm trying super-hard not to cry, but my voice is all trembly.

Mr Meaney shifts the rat to his other hand. "Well, Nellie," he says.

I look at his face. He doesn't look mad at all.

He doesn't look mean, either.

"I think you're very brave to tell me this." He smiles.

Ernesto is raising his hand. "Mr Meaney," he says. "I'm register monitor, but I really want to be rat monitor. Can I swap with Nellie?"

"That's very nice of you, Ernesto," says Mr Meaney. "What would you like to do, Nellie?"

I feel all mixed up inside. If I was brave enough to tell Mr Meaney the truth, maybe I'm brave enough to be rat monitor. I didn't hold a rat at Cute Critters, but I did watch Estella and Adam do it.

I take a deep breath. "I can be rat monitor," I tell Mr Meaney. I hold out my hands for the rat.

"Good for you," says Mr Meaney, as he hands me the rat. "I think you and Templeton will get along fine."

Templeton snuggles down in my cupped hands and closes his eyes. He feels warm and soft, not creepy at all! I can feel his heart beating. The light shines through his thin, pink ears. I can see the tiny veins. I'm holding a rat!

# Chapter 11

# Best first day ever

When it's finally lunchtime, my stomach is grumbling. I could eat a gazillion pieces of happy face toast.

Alexis is in front of me as we walk to the dinner hall. She looks hot and sweaty in her outfit. I'm glad I listened to Mum and wore my shorts. I wonder if her Mum or her nanny helped her decide what to wear.

"You really messed up your monitor job," she says.

Alexis is such a pain! "I thought you were going to get your dad to move you to Ms Anderson's class," I say.

"I changed my mind," Alexis says, looking down.

I think about what my friends said about Alexis – that she wants to be friends, but she doesn't know how.

"Do you want to sit with me at lunch?" Ashley asks me.

"Okay!" I say. "Do you want to sit with us, too?" I ask Alexis.

"Whatever," Alexis looks surprised. "I mean – yeah."

We sit with Ernesto and Brittany.

Ms Anderson's table is across from ours, and I wave at Estella, Jake and Adam. They raise their arms in a Worry Warriors sign and I smile.

I see Ashley looking at Ms Anderson's table, where Grace is sitting.

"I was really worried about not being in the same class as Estella, Adam and Jake," I say.

"Same for me and Grace," says Ashley.

"Hey, Nellie," says Brittany. "I'm afraid of rats, too."

"My big brother has a pet rat," says Ernesto, "and I play with it all the time."

"Thanks for saying you'd swap monitor jobs with me," I tell Ernesto. "I hope you don't mind that I kept it."

"It's okay," he says. "Maybe next time we'll swap jobs."

I feel good! It's going to be okay to have new friends in class. And I'll still see Estella, Adam and Jake at break, and before and after school.

"Hey, Ernesto," I say. "I have a joke you can use for taking the register." Then I whisper Henry's joke to Ernesto. "Raise your hand if you're not here!"

He nods and laughs. "Good one! Thanks."

Estella, Jake and Adam are waiting outside for me when I finish eating.

I tell them about the rat escaping and how I was brave enough to hold Templeton.

"Hooray!" they say together. We do another Worry Warriors knuckle tap before Adam runs off to play football and Jake goes to computer club in the ICT room.

"It's weird," I tell Estella as we walk around the playground. "I'm sad not to be in the same class as you and Jake and Adam, but I really like Mr Meaney."

The bell rings. We agree to walk home from school

together, and then I race back to Room Twelve.

Mr Meaney teaches a fractions lesson and gives work to do in our maths books.

I look up when I finish. Most of the children are still working. Mr Meaney waves his hand to signal me to come up to his desk. Uh-oh! Am I in trouble?

"I didn't get your *All About Me* assignment," he says.

"I didn't hand it in yet," I explain, "because it got smudgy where I rubbed stuff out. Is it okay to copy it out again?"

"Of course," he says.

Before I take it up to Mr Meaney, I add two things:

---

**14. My new friends are Brittany, Ashley, and Ernesto.**

---

**15. I am Room Twelve Rat Monitor.**

---

After I hand in my *All About Me* report, I swap my Meaney money for a free-reading book. It's the next book in my favourite new mystery series!

I settle into a beanbag chair in the reading corner. It's the best first day ever.

# ABOUT THE AUTHOR

**Marne Ventura** is the author of 29 children's books, 10 of them for Capstone. A former primary school teacher, she holds a master's degree in education from the University of California. When she's not writing, she enjoys arts and crafts, cooking and baking, and spending time with her family. Marne lives with her husband on the central coast of California. This is her first venture into fiction.

# ABOUT THE ILLUSTRATOR

Leo Trinidad is an illustrator and animator who has created many animated characters and television shows for companies including Disney and Dreamworks, but his great passion is illustrating children's books. Leo graduated with honours from the Veritas University of Arts and Design in San Jose, Costa Rica, where he lives with his wife and daughter. Visit him online at www.leotrinidad.com

# GLOSSARY

**archaeological dig**  the study of human life from long ago by uncovering old objects

**audiobook**  a recording of someone reading a book aloud

**courage**  bravery in times of danger

**duel**  a fight between two people with strict rules, usually caused by an insult

**dyslexia**  a learning disability that is usually marked by problems in reading, spelling, and writing

**eucalyptus**  a fragrant evergreen tree

**groomer**  a trained worker who washes and trims the hair and nails of dogs

**homeschool**  to teach children at home rather than in a school

**mannequin**  a life-sized dummy used to display clothes, usually in a shop window

**psychology**  the study of the mind, behaviour, and feelings

**scientific method**  a step-by-step process scientists use to solve problems

**sewer**  a system, often an underground pipe, that carries away waste

**smudge**  a dirty or blurry spot or streak caused by touching or rubbing it

**Viking**  a group of Scandinavian warriors who raided other European countries in the 8th to 10th centuries

**volunteer**  a person who does a job without pay

# TALK ABOUT IT

1. Nellie was really nervous about her first day of school, so she talked to her friends. What else might she have done?

2. Alexis is mean to Nellie when they meet at the Glam Kids shop. Nellie is there with her mother and Alexis is with her nanny. Talk about how Alexis might have felt about that.

3. Ernesto helped Nellie out when she had a problem in class and she helped him in return. What do you think Nellie learned from that?

# WRITE ABOUT IT

1. Think about a time you were worried about something. Write about how you felt and what you did to feel better.

2. Who is your favourite character in this story? Draw a picture of that person. Then write a list of five things you like about them.

3. How would you have helped Nellie with her worry? Think about that, and then write down what you would have done.

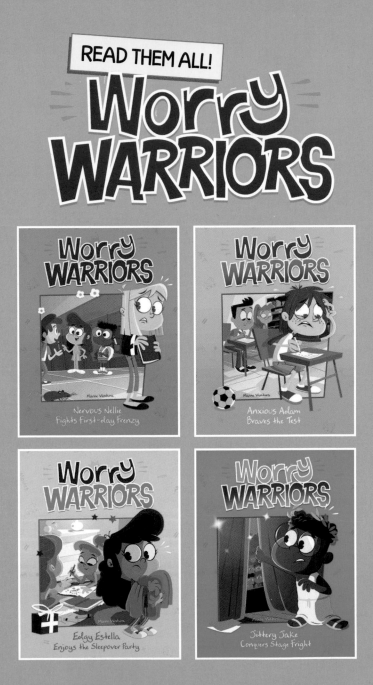